Christmas Magic

MICHAEL GARLAND

Dutton Children's Books • New York

Library of Congress Cataloging-in-Publication Data
Garland, Michael, date.
Christmas magic / by Michael Garland.—1st ed.
p. cm.
Summary: Emily builds a special snow-woman and joins
her and the new neighbor's snowman in a dance on a magical
Christmas Eve, when all sorts of amazing things happen.
ISBN 0-525-46797-1
[1. Christmas—Fiction. 2. Snowmen—Fiction.] I. Title.
PZ7.G18413 Ch 2001   [E]—dc21   2001025860

Published in the United States 2001 by Dutton Children's Books,
a division of Penguin Putnam Books for Young Readers
345 Hudson Street, New York, New York 10014
www.penguinputnam.com

Designed by Benjamin Wright

Printed in Hong Kong
First Edition
1 3 5 7 9 10 8 6 4 2

To my brother Thomas

Emily had always loved Christmas Eve, but this year something about it felt different. She couldn't tell quite what—maybe it was the way the snow glittered and danced as it drifted down from the sky. It seemed to her that the snowflakes had never been so perfect.

She watched the boy who was moving in next door. He seemed too shy to even say hello. A new friend would be nice, she thought, but he went inside before she could think of what to say.

Emily continued to roll the snowball she was forming and tried to imagine how her snow-woman would look when she was done.

She must have just the right name. Something fancier than mine, Emily thought as she balanced two more snowballs on top of the first one.
"I know—I'll call her Katrina!"

With an old coat and hat from the attic, a carrot from the pantry,

and some coal from the basement, Emily set to work. When she finished,
she stepped back to admire her snow-woman.

"Good night, my beautiful Katrina," she said softly. "It's getting late, and
I still have things to do."

Once inside, she carried her gifts—already wrapped and ribboned—to their place under the tree. Emily had finished her Christmas shopping weeks ago. She had picked out something special for Mother, Father, her cat, Ginger, and Max, her dog.

Next, she lifted the delicate angel choir from a cardboard box and carefully placed each figure on the round table. She glanced with anticipation at the empty stockings and then went upstairs to her room.

Emily changed into her cozy nightgown and looked out the window to check on Katrina. She was surprised to see the boy next door building a snowman in his front yard.

"I wonder what his name is," she whispered to Max and Ginger. She was tempted to call out the window to the boy, but she didn't want him to think she'd been spying.

Mother and Father tucked her into bed, turned out the light, and closed the door, but Emily was still wide awake. She couldn't help thinking about Katrina again. She climbed out of bed and crept to the window.

She was amazed by what she saw. Katrina's head was turned toward the snowman in the next yard. And his head was now tilted toward her. Emily knew it was impossible, but they seemed to be looking at each other.

Suddenly, Emily heard strange noises coming from the hall. She peeked around the door to see Ginger and Max, merrily meowing and barking out "Jingle Bells."

"How can this be?" Emily gasped.

A movement at the bottom of the stairs caught her eye. The angel choir had come to life! Emily bounded past her pets and down the steps.

The angels flew in circles and loop-the-loops, in and out of every room. Emily followed one of them right into the kitchen.

Emily stopped in the doorway. She was astonished to see an army of mice making Christmas pies. Mixing bowls, broken eggshells, and spilled sugar covered the kitchen table.

"Pets singing? Mice baking? What could be next?" Emily giggled. "This Christmas Eve really *is* different!"

From the kitchen, Emily went into the parlor. She was
just in time to see the Christmas stockings jump down from the fireplace
mantel and form a chorus line. With each kick, they spilled more of their
goodies onto the floor.

Then the Christmas tree started to spin slowly, as if to join in. All the ornaments floated loose from the branches. The presents rose from the floor and began circling the tree. That was when Emily heard the music coming from outside. She rushed to the window.

Katrina and the snowman weren't just looking at each other now—they were turning into real people! Of all the magical things Emily had seen, this was by far the most amazing. The snowman walked over to Katrina and bowed. She answered with a graceful curtsy.

Emily watched the dashing couple swoop and swirl over the glittering snow.
In one last sweep, they danced to the steps of her house.

Emily heard a light knocking and ran to the door. She was so excited she could hardly open it. There stood Katrina, radiant in her snowy gown. Emily smiled up at her.

"Hello, Emily," said Katrina. "We thought you might like to come outside and dance with us."

Emily nodded eagerly, then quickly put on her hat and coat, mittens, and boots.

Katrina and the snowman each took one of Emily's hands, and they leaped and swayed and twirled together over the moonlit snow.

When the snow stopped falling and dawn was near, Katrina looked up at the brightening sky. Emily followed her gaze.

"I loved dancing with you," Emily said breathlessly. "But I should go home now. Thank you for inviting me."

"Merry Christmas. We will never forget you," said Katrina, squeezing Emily's hand tightly in her own.

Once inside, Emily found she was too tired to climb the stairs. She snuggled up in the big chair by the Christmas tree and was soon fast asleep.

The next thing Emily knew, she felt a gentle shaking.
She sat up and looked around in bewilderment. The
stockings hung peacefully above the fireplace. The angels
stood exactly where she had placed them.

"Did the mice finish baking the pies?" she asked.

Father laughed. "That must have been some dream!"

Maybe I *did* dream the whole thing, she thought.
There's only one way to find out.

Emily pulled on her coat over her nightgown and
ran outside.

There, side by side on the sparkling snow, stood Katrina and the snowman.
The boy from next door was there, too.

"I can't believe it!" he whispered. "How did my snowman get all the way
over here?"

Emily grinned at him. "It was the Christmas magic," she whispered back.

Katrina and the snowman didn't say anything, but Emily was sure their
smiles were even wider than before.